NIGHTRIDER LUSTFUL CRAVING

MC EROTICA

CANDRA AUBREY

plicit Press
Erotica Fiction

CHAPTER 1 TROY BAXTER

"Oh, I love hearing stuff like that. I'm sure that design will definitely get on the cover of Newsweek," Heather said. She was trying to humor some poor bloke who thought that he was funny and who was raving to her about his designs. He begged for Heather to model for him, but that wasn't the type of life she led. In fact, the one thing that she wanted to do was get the hell out of here more than anything. It sounded like the perfect destiny for her, but alas, there were a few things not taken into account, that's for sure.

One of the big ones was the fact that she was born into this life. Heather Sampson was stuck trying to be something she totally was not. It was a problem that she didn't know how to fix. She tried to beg her parents to be normal, but coming from two millionaires made it that much harder; they ignored her pleas instead and they made her take stupid classes such as painting and violin lessons. Those weren't fun at all, and she didn't find them enjoyable whatsoever.

Heather had other issues as well. She didn't like the way things were run in her life either in some other ways. She was forced into an arranged marriage with a man that she didn't love at all, a prick named Justin Harrington. Justin was an asshole, for lack of a better word, and half the time she wanted to punch him in the face more than anything. Still, even though she would love to, it just wasn't an option, and that's where her problems got worse. Heather wanted to be free to choose whomever she wanted to date, but that would mean leaving this life and even being disowned by her parents. Although she loved the idea, in reality, it was a lot harder than that.

That's why she was here instead of doing other things. She had to pretend to give a shit about people that she hated and she had to make sure that she put on the best poker face imaginable. She hated her life sometimes, but the only way out was to play the game that they played, and sometimes you had to step in their shit to walk across the field.

Heather walked around and continued to talk to people, her 'friends' nearby, watching her with wary eyes. They all wanted the life that she had been given, and if it were possible, she'd gladly have given it to them. But alas, she had been born to it, so she had to do all of the things that she hated. One of the girls, a bright woman named Rachel who was only here because her mom was the teacher of the host, came by and looked at Heather up and down. Heather was in a white gown that came down to her feet, but everything else about her was plain. She had brown hair and hazel eyes and her hair was put up in a bun. That was a lot easier said than done, considering the fact that she had curly hair that didn't know how to stop being unruly. Rachel came over and gave Heather a fake smile before she spoke.

"So Heather, I heard that things are going great with you and Justin," she said.

"Sure. I guess," she replied. Heather hated talking about

that part of her life, but apparently, it was the only part that people gave a damn about. Nobody asked her about her grades or the sports that she played; instead, they wanted to know how the arrangements for the marriage were going. Heather was already 24 years old and she needed to be sent off to marriage soon. She was at the peak of her childbearing years, and it was only going to get harder from there. That wasn't the life she wanted to live, but she didn't know how to fix it.

"Why aren't you excited? I mean if I was banging a hot guy like Justin I would be," Rachel cooed.

The funny thing was that she hadn't done anything with him yet. Heather had decided to take things extra slow with Justin. When people asked, she responded with the stereotypical, "I wanted to make sure that he's the right guy for me." Or the other fun one, "I'm saving myself for marriage." Which was somewhat true, but the harsh reality was she hadn't found a man who'd been good enough for her to give away her v-card. She hated to say it, but it was true. She was very picky when it came to her sex life.

"I guess I am. I'm waiting for the right moment, and I want to take things slow," Heather replied.

"You're no fun."

With that, Rachel walked away. Heather sighed as she saw her tall, thin body walk away. She was so skinny, and she was completely enthralled with Justin. Yet Justin didn't seem to give two shits about her, instead, his eyes were on Heather the entire time. She had asked her mom and dad why she was going into this at one point, but they had simply said it was 'for the good of the family. Honestly, she felt like it was being used to fuck with her.

Heather walked around a little bit, not paying attention to where she was going. However, before she could stop herself she ran square into another guest, causing her to fall on her butt. She was about to get u and apologize when she realized who it was, and she took her apology back.

"Hey, there babe. How are you?" Justin asked.

Heather hated it when he called her that; she just didn't like it coming out of his mouth.

"Fine. What do you want?" she replied.

"That's no way to talk to the host of a party. I wanted to see how things were, especially with you," he replied. He was getting flirty and Heather was not in the mood for it. She tried to find a way out of this and after a moment saw the perfect opportunity to get away from him for the rest of the night.

"I'm okay. Just feeling a bit sick. If you'll excuse me," she said. She walked over to the restrooms outside of the main room that were attached to the front of the building. She got to the window and opened it, the cold breeze making her feel chilled. Normally she would never do this, but she had to get out of here. She climbed out the window, jumping to the ground and looking around. There wasn't a single soul around, so Heather decided to make a break for it. She made her way out of the mansion and down the street, trying to find a safe haven.

What she found was something, unlike anything she thought she would ever go into before. It was a biker bar and it looked a bit scary, to say the least. Heather opened the door and walked inside, and immediately the bartender scoffed.

"Get lost, Paris Hilton!" he said.

"Fuck off, Winston. Let her come in," another voice said as she stepped inside. Heather turned around and saw who it was, and immediately her jaw dropped.

He was the sexiest man she had ever seen. He had a

very tall frame, with long brown hair and beautiful green eyes. When he walked up to her he smiled and motioned over to the bar.

"Don't mind Winston, he can be a dick. Come with me," he said.

Heather followed him almost on instinct, her mind racing. This person was so sexy, and he was asking her to sit with him. When they got to the booth, he turned to her and smiled.

"You okay with a beer?" he asked.

She nodded and the man hollered at the bartender. She looked at him with a worried look before speaking.

"Umm who are you?" she asked. She had never met a guy this sexy before.

"I'm Troy Baxter. I'm a regular here. And you are?"

"Heather Sampson. I'm part of the infamous Sampson family," she replied.

"Ahh, those guys. Well hello there, Heather. I'm not going to judge you by your mommy or daddy's financial status. Plus you looked like you were trying to get the hell away from there. I wouldn't blame you though," he replied.

Heather chuckled as she relaxed. This man wasn't so bad, and thankfully he wasn't even trying to flirt with her. He seemed to have a whole lot more going for him as far as manners than Justin did, that's for sure.

"Yeah. I got stuck at this stupid party a friend of the family put on, and I needed to get out of there. So I climbed out the bathroom window and then made it here. I ran into you, and that was that" she explained.

"Wow, you're like a little warrior princess. In a good way," he replied.

Heather blushed at the flirting. She liked it a lot, even though normally she wanted to punch guys in the face who flirted with her at the drop of a pin. This guy seemed cool, and she did admire that about him.

"Well enough about me, what about you? You seem way different than a lot of the other people here," she stated.

Troy smiled at her and she could tell that he really did like having her around. After he cleared his throat, he started to speak. "Well, I'm part of a motorcycle gang. Or was. I left because I had some personal issues with them, but now I'm on my own. That means I get to have the fun of bar-hopping when I'm in cities like this. However, I'm kind of parked here for now. Mainly because it's a very nice place and Winston likes me," he replied.

Heather listened to this, enthralled by the mysterious man. He was so amazing, and he lived the dangerous life that she wanted. She would love to be a motorcycle babe, but she wasn't able to because of her parent's personal restrictions on everything in her life. However, hearing his stories got her excited, and it was like listening to a person telling war stories.

However, Heather wanted to know more about the issues. That might be where the real juicy story was, and she would love to hear that.

"So what happened with the guys? What were the issues?" she asked.

The man immediately froze up, and Heather wanted to take back what she said. It was a very stupid mistake, and she didn't want him to be mad at her. However, after a minute he spoke again.

"I would rather not get into those. However, you seem very different than the others," he replied. He liked how weird this chick was. Even though he really just saw her as a woman who needed some companionship, he did like listening to her. Plus she had a great set of knockers, and that didn't hurt either.

"Well, I would love to be free. I feel like my entire life is being judged based on if I follow in my parent's footsteps or not. It's completely annoying," she replied.

"Ahh. That sucks," he said.

"You're telling me," she stated. She would love to just get rid of that life forever and be free. However, talking to him certainly made her feel that, even though he didn't seem to be in the same boat as her. After a few more drinks, they were both a little bit inebriated.

"I should call a cab," she said.

"Nah, it's cool. I'll drive you home," he replied.

Heather looked at him with a shocked expression. "You do realize you're drunk right? I don't want to go with you on your bike if you're like that," she replied.

"True. Call the cab," he said. He wanted to tell her that he drove buzzed all the time, but he didn't want her to feel sad. After a few minutes, the cab came by and took her to the apartment that she stayed at when she was in the city. The mansion was out of the city limits, and right now the last thing that she wanted to do was to see her parents. That was going to be annoying.

After they got home, Heather unlocked the door and let him in; she had never let a guy in her house before who looked as good as him, and already she could feel herself getting turned on.

"Damn you sure have a nice—"

Before he could respond, she crushed her lips against his. The kiss was heated and passionate and while Troy kissed her, he closed the door. Heather loved this, and she continued to kiss him long and hard. The make-out session was wet and sloppy, and he definitely liked it that way.

Heather had never done something so daring before. She had kissed a guy a few times and she did give a blowjob once, but that was her entire repertoire of sexual experiences. Yet with this man, she wanted it all. She pinned him up against the wall and continued to kiss him hard, loving the way his lips felt against hers.

Heather started to let him take over, and he pushed his tongue right against hers, massaging with her lips; she was already getting wet from the touch. Heather knew about that, and most of the time she settled the craving by masturbating, but this was much better than some little toy.

Troy loved kissing her, even if it was just for the feeling of pleasure. However, she wanted something else. He led her to the bedroom and laid her down, pulling off the gown. Immediately Heather gasped as he exposed her big breasts, which were like giant white orbs just waiting for him to suck on them.

"Damn you have nice breasts," he said. Heather loved the way he said that as his lips trailed down to where one of the nipples was. Before Heather could say anything, he took one in his mouth while his other hand started to caress and play with the other lonely nipple. It was fun to see her squirm, for it was such a turn-on to see a woman like that. He also knew that Heather wasn't that sexually experienced, so he wanted to give her the best damn feelings that he could give.

He started to suck on the nipple harder, causing her to moan in pleasure and throw her head back in ecstasy. She loved it so much, and she could feel the wetness start to pool up inside of her. Even though he hadn't even fucked her yet, she was about to cum.

However, Troy noticed it and immediately pulled away,

smiling at her. Heather was already very sexually frustrated, so when he stopped she got annoyed, to say the least.

"Why'd you stop?" she asked. She loved how it felt, and he was so perfect with his movements against her skin. It was as if a small fairy was ghosting against it, and feeling his touch made her moan in pleasure in ways she never thought that she would before.

Troy simply smiled at her before he continued on, moving his lips down her breasts right to her stomach. Yet instead of kissing it, he moved his tongue up and down her stomach, drawing shapes with that muscle. It was so erotic and sexy that Heather was turned on once again. She didn't know she could ever be so enthralled with a man like she was now. This certainly explained why all of her friends had lost their virginity way before she did. She didn't know this kind of pleasure had even existed, but she knew now, thanks to this man.

He moved his lips down to where her pussy was and instead of fingering it, he pushed his lips into her hole and snaked his tongue out, exploring the wet area. He started to massage her overhead with his tongue, and Heather felt like she was going crazy. She arched her back and Troy took the chance to move his tongue slowly over the roof, soon finding her sweet spot. When he did, Heather went crazy, thrashing around as he continued to hit just the right place. After a few more times of grazing over it, Heather's pussy tightened around his tongue, causing her to cum.

Troy loved seeing her like this, and it was fun seeing a girl who hadn't really experienced pleasure before getting a taste of it. He started to move away and undo his pants, pulling it off to reveal his hard cock. It was already twitching for her, and she looked at it with pure desire and want. It looked great, and as she licked her lips she imagined what it was going to feel like. Troy made her personal desires a reality very soon though, and when he did she experienced a pleasure better than anything she had experienced before.

He pushed himself deep into her pussy, making her scream out in pleasure. Troy didn't know she was a virgin and for a split second, it hurt. However, he made the pain go by capturing her lips in a passionate kiss. Heather moaned in pleasure as he did this, loving the way it felt. As he continued to thrust into her, Heather gasped. She loved the way it felt, she definitely did feel like a goddess, and she felt the ultimate pleasure with this man.

He continued to thrust into her hard, but the tightness of her pussy brought him close. After a few more strokes he screamed out, spilling his seed into her. Heather let out a moan as well as her own pussy walls tightened up around him. It felt so nice releasing again, and the second time was better than the first.

After he finished up, he lay next to her and Heather cuddled up to him. They soon fell asleep, both of them happy and satisfied. Little did they know, however, that the peace was only fleeting and soon things were going to get even crazier.

CHAPTER 2 THE NEXT MORNING

The next morning Heather woke up and saw Troy. Immediately the feelings from last night came back and she liked that quite a lot, even though it would take some getting used to. Yet she did have a few questions for him, and she did want to get to know him better. It was as if she was an open book, and he was one that was locked uptight. She wanted to find out more about him more than anything, and she was going to do it whether he liked it or not.

Troy started to rouse a little bit, his eyes flickering a tiny bit. It was adorable to see, and Heather wanted to go out and touch one of those eyelashes. As she did though, he woke up, startling her.

"Jesus!" she said.

He smiled and looked at her, giving her a peck on the cheek. She flushed when she felt it, liking it a whole lot more than she expected.

"Hey there. Did you sleep okay?" he asked.

"I did. You?"

"Great. Better than I have in a long time," he replied.

Heather smiled, but there was something eating away at her that she had to get off her chest. She had to talk to him about last night, for it was something that did bother her a whole lot and she wanted to make sure that he knew where she stood on it.

"So about last night..."

Troy looked up and smiled at her with that trademark coy smile that seemed to make her go crazy with both lust and worry. She wanted to find out more about him, and she certainly did feel like there were many questions left unanswered.

"What about it? I had a lot of fun, and I'm sure that you did as well. I know you did," he replied. Heather blushed at the way he talked to her, her body growing excited once again. She really wished she could tell him what was on her mind, but it did make her worry a tiny bit. However, she did have the thought that if this weren't in the open, she would go crazy.

"Well, I wanted to think about us. I mean you're really cute, but I don't want to be some sort of fuck toy. That's not the kind of life that I like. What do you think?" she asked. She hated sounding so stupid when she asked questions like this, but it was what was eating her mind.

He simply smiled at her, shaking his head. "I agree. But I think we can talk about that later," he replied. Troy was slow to answer, and although that did help in some regards, in others it was simply maddening.

Heather didn't want to delay; she just wanted to enjoy the moment. However, after about a minute there was a knock on the door. Heather got up, wrapping a towel around her body and walking over to the door.

"I really hope this isn't my mother," she said. However,

when she opened it, another sight appeared that she thought would never show up.

It was Justin, and he had a bouquet of flowers in his hand and a big smile on his face.

"Hey there baby, I brought you flowers!"

CHAPTER 3 SHOCK

Heather was in shock. She wanted to get this guy out of her life, but that was a lot harder than she thought, apparently. He was standing right there and after a moment, Troy poked his head out.

"Who's that?" he asked.

"Nobody," Heather replied.

"Oh, just her fiancée," Justin cooed. Heather flashed him a dirty look, annoyed by this shit.

"What the hell do you want? I told you not to bother me," she said. She looked at him with a set of glaring eyes, and Justin simply smiled.

"I just wanted to give flowers to you. However, I think you already have someone else who's deflowered your body. No worries though, I know that he doesn't have as much money as I do," he replied. Justin loved to brag about his money, and that was the biggest turn-off for Heather. She didn't give two shits if the guy had two dollars to his name or two million dollars; she based what she wanted on love and desire.

"Fuck off," she replied.

"Oh gladly. I hope things are good with your little lover boy back there," Justin said. Before he could leave, however, a presence came up behind Heather, shrouding her with a dark shadow.

"Hey there. I am the other guy. And I think she told you to fuck off. Now if you don't mind, I suggest you do that before you see me and what I would love to do to that faggoty little face of yours," Troy said.

Justin backed away. "Well excuse me, princess. I guess I'll be going," Justin replied. He ran away and Heather threw the flowers in the garbage bag, annoyed as shit at what Justin did to her. It was super embarrassing, and it annoyed her that the fucker didn't know when to quit. Why did she have to tell him 'no' forty times?

"What the fuck was that? I thought you weren't seeing a guy," he said.

Heather looked at him with her mouth open, about to explain. "It's very complicated. So, my parents arranged a marriage for me. But the guy they chose is a fucking dunce. I hate him so much, but they don't seem to understand that. I told them at least three times that I didn't want to get married but they ignored it and they keep pushing this arranged marriage crap on me. Ugh, it's so annoying but I don't know what to do about it. I can't stand it though," she replied. It was the only way she could explain herself and save face with Troy.

"Really? There's still doing that arranged marriage crap in this day and age?" he asked.

"Sadly yes. They think that they should stick to tradition. I left last night because he was being obnoxious, and I couldn't stand it," she replied. It was the truth, but Troy still gave at her with a look of disdain.

"I can't believe you though. Why didn't you tell me this?"

"Because I didn't think you would believe me! Plus I wasn't completely aware last night after I had all those drinks. Plus, do you think that I'm just going to introduce myself and say 'Hey, I'm Heather, and I have a psychotic guy who thinks I'm his fiancée following me. Oh, and I want to fuck you.' Do you really expect me to say that outright, because if you do you're as stupid as I am?" she replied. It was the truth, and she hated to say it but that's what she was thinking.

Troy was shocked at how rude this woman could be. Yet at the same time, he found it sexy. He had to do a bit of thinking though. Although he did believe her, it was still a bit scary, to say the least.

"I think I'm going to go. You'll know where to find me. Plus, I feel like I'm being watched," he replied. He started to walk away and immediately Heather grew a bit wary. Why was this guy caring so damn much about if he was being watched or not? He didn't seem like the type who would give a shit about something like that.

"What do you mean there is something there? Of course, there is, it's called the environment," she replied. She hated sounding like such a smartass, but it's the truth. He was freaking out over nothing, and it was starting to get annoying.

However, before Heather could explain herself, even more, Troy walked away, leaving her alone. She didn't know what to do at this point except wait and see, for she had a lot of things to talk to him about, but it didn't seem like the right time to say it. She knew where he was, and she would go there if needed. Right now, she needed to think about a few things.

However, despite him leaving she wished she had asked him to stay, for he seemed like exactly the person she needed in her life. However, she needed a break to think about things, especially the risk she was about to take.

CHAPTER 4 WEEKS

A couple of weeks had passed since the whole incident and although she didn't really like to think about how shitty her life was, it seemed to be the only thing on her mind these days. She wished that she didn't have such a crappy situation, but it was the only thing she knew how to do. Sure, she went to college, but that didn't mean jack shit in some cases, and most of the time people didn't want to hire her because they already thought that she was getting a ton of money from her parents. That left her trying to live her fake life, but even that was getting too hard for her.

Her parents were pissed about what she had done, and that was putting it lightly. They had actually grounded her and made her go to a bunch of social events because of it. She hated them, but she was very good at pretending to give a shit about people. She talked with all of them, and they considered her to be a fine and charming young lady, even though she was far from it. Really nice though, and that made things a whole lot better for her later on. Plus it seemed like after a while her mom and dad stopped caring about what she did, and this led to her being able to finally get back to the life that she wanted to have.

She thought about the best way to get away from them, yet she was still wary. She did want to be free, but she didn't want her freedom to be wasted on someone who thought she wasn't good enough for him. She did really like Troy, but she was worried that he only saw her as a sexy woman and not as anything more. As much as she wanted to think otherwise, it was starting to get harder for her. He had never visited her after that night, and Heather was starting to think that she had ruined her chances with him. She didn't like the idea that she had lost her virginity to him, but she knew that her mistake was hers to bear. She would just have to go on and continue living; there wasn't anything that she could do about it now.

One night, she was made by her parents to go to another one of Justin's fucking parties. She was so sick of them, but she did have to stay on her mom and dad's good side. When she got there she was bored as hell, and that was putting it nicely. She walked around the place, looking at all the people and then realizing that she was the loner. It seemed like everybody was chummy with each other, while she was stuck on the outside looking in. She hated it, she didn't know what to do about it. She was different from them, for she didn't think this was the life that she wanted to live, and instead she wanted to be free like other people. That was what she wanted, but others didn't understand the pain that she went through.

After about an hour Heather felt a presence behind her, and she turned around. Much to her dismay, it was Justin. Instead of his trademark smile, he had a frown on his face.

"Glad to see you could make it. Where's the boy? Or is

he too scared to show up at a fancy dinner party?" Justin teased.

"Fuck off. If you have nothing nice to say then go talk to a tree or something. I'm sure they would love to hear your jeers," Heather replied. She wasn't that good at comebacks, but if it made him go away and leave her to her own devices, then that was better than anything.

"Oh, don't be so harsh. I don't mind that you wasted your virginity on some broke fag. And to think that he called me one of those. Oh please, it's not like I'm trying to be some loser like him," he replied.

Heather wanted to punch him in the face. However, she was in a very fancy setting, and she had to save face with him.

"What do you want?" she asked.

Justin smiled and grew closer to her, smiling warmly. "I want you."

Heather moved back, disgusted by this man. She hated talking to him, and the fact that he tried to use that move on her sickened her even more. She tried to find a way out of it, but it was a lot harder than she thought.

"Why are you doing this? You know I don't want you."

"You may say that now Heather, but I'm sure that you won't be saying that when mommy and daddy find out that you fucked a stranger. That's what he is right? A complete fucking stranger," the guy said.

Heather was seething. She didn't think that Troy was a stranger at all. Even though they barely knew each other and only knew about each other's bodies, she did feel something strong with him that was better than anything she had ever felt before with a man. This guy wasn't going to get the best of her, and she was going to prove it to him.

"You're wrong. You're a stranger in my eyes. I have to pretend to be in love with you to make people happy. In reality, you're a weird slime ball who will probably never get laid even if you paid out a billion dollars. You don't understand Justin, you're nothing but a lowlife who uses other people and tempts them with money. It sickens me, and maybe you could take a lesson from Troy. I didn't fuck him because he has oodles of money or lives in a very nice house. I could care less where he lives, but frankly, he made me feel something I've never felt before. If I was with you, I could never feel it. I'm sorry to break it to you Justin, but that's the truth."

Before Justin could say anything, Heather ran away and immediately ran to the bathroom. It was raining hard outside, but she didn't care. What she needed was a release, some form of solace that she could get for herself. That was what mattered in her life, and she definitely felt like she could get it by leaving this place and seeing him.

She took off her shoes and started to run with them in tow, the rain soaking her strapless dress. It was pretty short already, but as she continued to run in the rain, it soaked her even more. She shivered at the cold feeling, but she didn't care. She just loved how it felt and nothing was going to stop her.

Heather never got to play in the rain like other kids, so this was something new to her. She felt like jumping around, moving fast and swiftly through the puddles. When she got to the street, she ran down it to where the bar was. When she got in there Troy was right at the bar, smiling excitedly when he saw her.

Heather was soaking wet, and he loved it. He always thought it was sexy when women were wet, but with

Heather, it was even better. Her dress clung to her and she had water droplets coursing down her body. Her nipples were showing through the dress, a sign that she wasn't wearing a bra.

"Well hello there," he said.

"Hey," she simply replied.

"Come up to the bar. I think we need to have a little talk," he said.

Winston rolled his eyes but got them both beers, setting them down in front of them. Heather thanked him and took a sip, and Troy looked her up and down.

"You look like you ran away from another party," he stated. It was the only thing he could think of saying. Heather blushed at this comment, even though it was probably the truth.

"Is it that obvious?"

"Not because of the rain, because of the look in your eyes. You have the same petrified look on your face. Like you're going to piss off people if you do this," he explained.

"Well I already did that," she replied.

"I guess what's done is done. Now you're with me, so I don't think anything bad will happen to you," he cooed. Heather liked the way his voice sounded, and she did feel excited when she heard that. After Winston gave them, another round Troy looked at her with a mischievous look on his face.

"Say, do you want to come with me? I have a surprise waiting for you," he said.

"What kind of surprise?"

Heather looked at him with a curious look. She liked surprises a lot, and this man certainly had a whole lot up his sleeve. After a second, he smiled at her before standing up.

"Well the only way to find out is to come with me," he stated. Heather decided to follow him. What was the worst that could happen anyway? They went out of the bar through the back way until they were in a back alleyway.

"What are we..."

Before Heather could ask, Troy's lips were on hers. They crushed their lips together and Heather felt him start to snake his tongue in. They were getting soaked out there, but Heather didn't care. She liked how rough this was. It was the sexiest thing she'd ever done, and she didn't regret this at all

She was a bit worried though about Winston coming out, and after a moment pulled away, looking at him with a panted gasp.

"Do you think Winston will see us?" she asked.

"No. He doesn't give a damn as long as it's not in front of the bar. Trust me, I've walked out to weirder things happening out here before," he replied.

Heather nodded and started to kiss him again, the pleasure coursing through her body and the passion increasing between the two of them. It was the best feeling, and Heather knew that she was free when she kissed him. It was so different from any other time she'd done anything with a man. Her parents had tried to set her up with some of the guys that they were friends with, but most of them didn't click. They had only forced the whole Justin thing on her became she hadn't agreed to any of their other choices. It was as if the gods were punishing her because she didn't like him. But she didn't give a damn. All she wanted was to be with Troy. She would do anything right now to have that, and so would Troy.

They continued to kiss each other hard, both of them

loving the way the other felt. Troy opened his mouth and Heather pushed her tongue in, loving the way it felt. She was so turned on that Troy immediately started to push the bottom of her dress up, slipping his cold and wet hand into her panties and fucking her with his fingers.

"Fuck," she said softly as he continued to do this. She was going crazy, and he loved it. Troy loved seeing a woman go mad for him, and he knew that Heather was already mad for him in many different ways. He continued to do this hard, pushing his wet finger in deeply and feeling her warm pussy. He immediately found her pleasure spot, and after pushing his finger against that, she moaned.

While he did that, he moved his lips up against the clothed breast. He started to suck on the nipple through the fabric and Heather moaned, her back arching against the wall in pleasure. She had never felt something so erotic before, and as he did this, she could feel herself going mad. After a bit Troy wanted to touch them, so he pulled the top of the dress down with his mouth and immediately latched onto her breast while his free hand started to play with the other.

Heather was on cloud nine and couldn't help but love the pleasure that completely and utterly took her over. It was like she was going crazy, and she felt like she wasn't going to come down from the high that she was on. After a few more thrusts, however, her pussy walls tightened against his digit as she came, her release coming out of her body.

After he finished that, he pushed his finger into Heather's mouth and she licked it erotically. Troy loved that, and once he finished he flipped her so that her chest was against the wall. Her nipples were hard from the cold rain and the wall and while she shuddered at that Troy pushed his cock in, sliding it deep into her.

He started to go slowly, but after a couple more thrusts, he started to move faster and faster. He started to thrust harder, and Heather gasped in pleasure at the feeling. He was getting in deeper and deeper, her body going crazy and her pussy quivering at the feeling of his cock taking her.

After he thrust a few more times, he knew he was spent. He was so turned on when he saw her that already he was leaking precum while he fingered her. He started to go all-out, pushing his dick harder and harder into her wet body, penetrating her in a way she'd never felt before. It was deeper than the first time, and Heather liked it a whole lot. It was so different, but at the same time so erotic, that she felt like she was going to explode in pleasure.

After a few more thrusts Troy pushed in deeper, moaning in pleasure as he felt his seed release from his body and fill her up. Heather was about to cum too, and after another thrust her pussy tightened against his throbbing cock and released her essence while he came into her. It was amazing, and she was completely and utterly in bliss that she never felt before.

After he finished up, he pulled out of her, smiling happily. "So what did you think?" he asked.

"It was...amazing," she managed to reply. She was still trying to get back down from heaven and the high level of bliss that she just reached. It turned out to be a whole lot harder than she thought.

"Well, I'm glad. Tell you what, why don't we go inside and talk a little bit? I have a couple of personal things to discuss with you. Just in regard to what we should do next."

Heather nodded and followed him like an obedient dog. She fixed her dress back up as she walked into the restaurant, trying not to flush from the feeling that she had regarding how she looked. She finally had Troy, and it seemed like he wanted her as well. Things were already forgetting about Justin and his bullshit. She knew whom she wanted, and that was going to be Troy. He was her sweet bad boy, and she was ready for him to take her.

CHAPTER 5 THE INCIDENT

When they got inside Winston looked at them as if they were crazy.

"What the hell were you doing?" he asked.

Troy flashed Winston a smile that is both devilish and mysterious. Winston couldn't help but laugh as Troy and Heather went back to the bar. After a minute or so, Troy turned to Heather with a smile on his face.

"So you're probably wondering what in the world the plan is at this point," he stated.

"That would be nice to know, honestly. I mean I'm wondering what you want to do about it," she said. She did want to stay with him, but it was going to be weird for a little while since she was in the position where her parents were still controlling things.

"Well, I was thinking we could go on an adventure. I was planning on leaving this place. As much as I love it, I feel like I have to move on. I have some personal business to handle in another place as well," he said.

Heather wondered what he meant by that, and she did

want to find out what it meant. "What do you mean? What kind of personal business?" she said.

"Well, I do have to handle something in Arizona. It's pretty complicated, but that's where my old gang is. There was a small incident, and they told me to go into hiding while they tried to iron it out. That didn't work as well as it might have, but I think it would be safe to head on back. It's complicated to explain, but over time I think I'll be able to talk about it," he replied.

Heather looked at him with a wary glance. She did want him to be honest with her, but he was still being some-what elusive in what he said.

"Will I find out eventually?" she asked.

"Yes, you will. I assure you that one day, when things are better, you'll find out then. For now, I want to know if you want to come with me. It'll be a fun adventure together, and we'll be able to not only go there but to other places as well," he replied.

Heather thought about this for a second and immedi-ately grew excited. She did want to see the world, and she wanted to be free more than anything. Even though he was being elusive now, she knew that things would get better over time.

"I would love to," she replied.

"Good. Do you want to leave tonight?"

"Sure. Sounds fine to me," Heather said. She didn't care if it pissed off her family. She was ready to have a new life.

"Good. So I guess we'll head to your place and then bounce." Heather nodded and got up, walking with him to the bike. The rain had stopped, but that was the least of their problems. When they got outside, Troy gasped at his bike. It was scratched up, and the tires were flattened. However, the real danger was on the front of the bike.

Scratched in the red paint in jagged letters was the word, "Traitor," and Troy immediately knew what it meant.

CHAPTER 1

HEATHER LOOKED at the mess in front of her. Someone really had it out for them, and it wasn't going to be pretty. However, she had to keep calm. There was no way she was going to flip out on him just yet. She needed to figure out what to do first, along with getting more information on this man and why all this had happened.

"Who did this...?" he said. Heather watched as Troy fell to the ground, his body shaking. He didn't appear to know what was going on either, and that's what scared Heather the most. She knew there were some secrets that this man wanted to keep from her, and she knew the only way to continue to be with him is to find out the truth.

"You mean you don't know who did it either?" she asked. It worried her a tiny bit that she was with this man but he didn't understand the whole issue either. She felt like she was running around blindly with him instead of really knowing exactly what she was getting into.

"I don't. I've never had this happen to me before. I want to know who the fucker is so I can beat the shit out of him, but I still don't have any clue as to why they would do something like this," he replied.

Heather felt completely lost. She was with a man who had issues of his own, but he didn't even know what to do about them. It didn't feel safe for her to be here, and that was what went through Heather's mind as she looked at Troy and the worrisome look he had on his face. She thought about how to say it, but it was Troy who took the words right out of her mouth.

"You don't feel safe around me, do you? You seem scared. I would be too if I were you," he simply said. His head hung down in shame, and Heather was in shock. She hated how he looked. Heather took a step closer, but when she got up to him he put her hand up.

"Just... let me be for a bit. I have to be alone right now. Why don't you just head on home?" he asked. He seemed so broken that Heather wanted to help him. But she could tell that he didn't want anything to do with her or their relationship. He needed some space, and frankly Heather wanted to be alone as well to think about everything and try to figure out the best course of action to take at this point.

"Okay. Well here's my number if you want to talk. I don't want to leave you," she said. The truth was Heather did want to leave this place, to get out of here before it got too dangerous and she got in over her head.

"Thanks. I don't want to hurt you Heather, but I feel like for right now I need some time alone. I might call you later, but if you don't' hear from me don't feel bad. I'm sorry that I can't drive you back up there. I'm not really in the best condition mentally or physically to do that right now," he replied.

Heather nodded and before she left she planted a kiss on his cheek. He flinched, but accepted it.

"I hope you feel better. I'll see you around," Heather simply said. She walked away, leaving Troy alone with his bike. It was such a pathetic sight to see, and she hated seeing him so broken. Yet at the same time, she felt like she had made it out of there before it was too late, and that's what really mattered to her. Although she did care about Troy a whole lot, she didn't know if that was the best thing for her right now.

When she got back to the mansion, the party was starting to wind down and the guests were going home. At this point, Heather's dress was mostly dry, and her hair was tied up in a tight bun to hide the wetness of it. She had to at least try to look like a civilized human being. She placed her shoes back on her feet and went back up to where the party was happening, opening the back door and slinking back in.

It seemed like she hadn't missed anything of vital importance. Her mother and father were talking to some people, neither of them really giving a shit about what their daughter did. When she did walk in her mother flashed her a dirty look, a sure sign that she knew exactly where she had run off to. Heather wasn't in the mood to get into a fight with her mother about this just yet, so she decided to lay low for a while before she tried to do anything else.

She walked up to where the lounge was, grabbing a glass of champagne and sipping it on it. The people seemed so fake, yet she knew this was where she was supposed to be. This was what made her parents happy, and it wasn't getting any better. However, she knew that the life that she wanted to live was nothing but a dream that she would never have, and the harsh reality was that she needed to just deal with the cards she had been dealt and try to find the best solution for getting over it. Heather had the rest of her life ahead of her anyway, she could always find someone better. Plus, she would inherit her parent's inheritance when they passed on, and they were able to supply her with anything that she wanted. Yet the only thing that she did want at this point was the life that she had with this mysterious man. It was something that she really wanted, even though it was considered unconventional in many different ways.

Heather sat there trying to mull over her life in the peace and quiet of the house. Thankfully a lot of the guests were gone, and she didn't have to put on a fake face for some of the bigwigs that usually came through these parties in an attempt to hang out and find the next best successors for their shitty companies. She just wanted to ride away, to get the hell out of here and go to Arizona with Troy. That was all she wanted, and that was what she craved more than anything. The idea of freedom sounded so enticing to her, but she knew that it was a dream that she would never have.

Heather sighed, trying to figure out what to do next. Out of the corner of her eye, she saw someone that she would love to punch in the face. It was Justin, and he was still in that damned white suit that looked like shit on him. She could see the smug look on his face as he looked at her, and immediately he made a beeline for the couch that she sat on. He looked at her with a leering grin, and Heather tried her best to cover her body with her arms. Justin looked at her with malice on his face, and Heather knew this was going to be one hell of a long night.

"Hey there. I'm shocked that you're still here. I thought you ran off to your little boy toy. It's kind of cute really, that you should try to ditch me for a man like that. I think you're way out of his league if I do say so myself," he cooed. He was starting to move closer, and although Heather was disgusted, she also knew that this was what she had to do.

She had to pretend to like this guy, to think he was the most attractive man ever, but in reality, she just wanted to run away from there and never come back again.

"If you're here to gloat, then I suggest that you fuck off," Heather replied simply.

"Ooh, a feisty one. No matter, I know that the woman would love to come back to me anyway," he said. He wigged his eyebrows and immediately Heather wanted to just roll her eyes and look away. This guy was trying way too hard to get her attention, and although most girls would find it cute as hell, she wanted to punch him in the face even more after all of that.

"Yes, I am. Now, what the hell do you want?" Heather asked.

"I thought you would never get to that point, Heather. I like the way you think baby. Plus I have something that you don't have," he replied.

"What? I only came back because I forgot my purse," Heather lied. She had had it with her the entire time, but she needed to figure out a way to get him off her back.

"Bullshit. I saw you leave with it. You can't fool me, baby, because I know that you're not that smart. Unlike me, who's a boy genius."

Heather had to keep her cool, but it was starting to get to her badly. She would love to wipe the smile off his face by just giving him a good, hard slap, but she had to stand her ground and hope that he would leave her alone. After a few moments, however, she heard him speak again.

"Well the thing is Heather, I don't think your mommy and daddy approve of you going out with a guy like that. I know that's true because they told me to stop you from being with him. However, I was thinking of the best way to convince you so that you could be safe and I could get what

I want. I am your fiancée after all, so I have the intention of both your parents and my parents in mind as well. They want us to get married, so I'm going to make a proposal," he started.

Heather looked at him in worry. What the hell does he mean by that?

"What is it?"

Justin smiled and came closer, his nasty mouth near the shell of her ear. "Fuck me and I'll make sure your parents don't find out what you were really doing tonight," he cooed.

Heather was disgusted. There was no way she was going to lose herself and give in to this man. However, when she thought of the situation she was in, there was no way she could get out of it. She had to follow his wishes, and she needed to do so fast. She knew that her mom and dad were pissed at her, but the only way to quell that was to give in to this man. It disgusted her to stoop this low, but it might be for the best. After all, she didn't know where Troy and she stood anymore.

"Fine."

"Good. Besides, you need to forget about Troy, baby. He's going to leave you anyway. I know exactly how those guys work. They only want to fuck you for the moment and then leave. I'll stick around though honey," he said.

The words that came out of his mouth sickened her, but she nodded. He got up and extended his hand and Heather grasped it, trying to not look so displeased. She had to put on a fake front for him, even though a part of her wanted nothing to do with this and would love to just wipe the smirk off his face.

They walked into his bedroom and he closed the door, locking it. Heather had been in here multiple times, but this time it was different. It was almost like he had planned it, with the candles around and the heart petals on the bed.

Before she could think of anything else, however, she felt his lips press onto hers in a fervent kiss. It took Heather by surprise, but she knew that to get him off her back she would have to comply with his personal desires. He started to kiss her harder and Heather gave in. Even though he was a creep, he was a decent kisser. Probably from all the experience he had kissing and necking with the other whorish girls that he loved to play around with. Faithful, her butt.

They started to deepen the kiss even more, and Heather left her mouth open for a moment. Justin took that opportunity and started to snake his tongue into her wide mouth, mingling it with hers and running it over the roof of her mouth. His breath reeked of champagne, but she knew that hers wasn't that much better. They continued to kiss hard until Justin pushed her down on the bed, getting on top of her and smiling excitedly.

"Let's see what you're hiding underneath this sexy little dress of yours," he said. He started to peel it off of her, revealing her naked breasts and her small thong. Immediately Justin's cock grew even harder with desire, and he immediately grew excited at the way she looked.

"Damn, no wonder guys like your body. You have the tits of a goddess," he said. Heather rolled her eyes at the cheesy comment, but then she started to moan as Justin started to suck on her nipples and play with the little buds with his free hand. His other hand started to pull on the bun, causing a small yelp to escape her as he pulled it out roughly. She wanted to slap him for the pain he caused her, but he pushed her down, pinning her there. She couldn't escape, and she knew that she would have to go through with this even though she would rather die than fuck this man.

Of course, dying would be a bit of an issue at this point. She wanted to see Troy again, and the entire time he was sucking on the little buds and nibbling on her little areolas, she thought of Troy. That was the only way to make it more bearable in her mind, and Justin smiled. He thought he was arousing her, but in reality, when she did all of this, the only thing on her mind was Troy. That was who she wanted, not this son of a bitch who thought that trying to get her to give into him was okay.

Still, she couldn't back out now. She needed to see Troy again and she would sacrifice a part of herself to do so. She still felt a tinge of doubt, her mind wondering what had happened to Troy after they parted. When Justin moved his hands down to her pussy and started to play with it while his other hand took off her panties though, she immediately started to moan. It did feel good, but it wasn't the thing that she wanted. She wanted Troy, and that's who she really desired.

Justin started to undo his pants, pulling them down along with his boxers and then quickly discarding them. His throbbing cock was ready for her, and before she could say anything he pushed himself into her slowly, savoring the feeling of her tight hole. Justin was annoyed he didn't get to take her virginity, but this was definitely the next best thing.

He started to thrust in and out of her hard, each time causing Heather to almost yelp at the feeling. It wasn't much fun, and it did hurt a little bit. But she wasn't able to do anything except endure it. It did feel good in a way, but it wasn't as fun as the sex that she had with Troy. This was so vanilla and boring that she almost fell asleep at one point, but she needed to fake the moans in order to get Justin excited. She started to moan even more, trying her best to sound like she was about to fake an orgasm. Justin loved hearing this, and he knew that she was close. He was getting there as well, and after a few more thrusts he let out a low groan as his body went completely crazy.

Heather let out a final moan as she pretended to have her big orgasm. It wasn't anything special, but it surely did convince Justin. He let out one last moan as he came, his seed shooting into her. It didn't feel as comforting as it did when Troy came, and Heather didn't really like how it felt. Still, she had to pretend for her sake, and for the sake of her future relationship with Troy. She might have been afraid before, but she knew now what she wanted.

After he finished up, he pulled out and they lay there. Heather was tired, but she knew that she had to go home. Still, she really didn't have a way to get there until later on that night. She started to fall asleep there, her mind thinking about what to do next. Even though she was nervous about talking to Troy again, she knew she would have to do it, for it did make her feel better just knowing that there was something out there for her.

Heather knew what she wanted, and she would talk to Troy again tomorrow.

CHAPTER 2

THE NEXT MORNING Heather woke up, trying to think about what to do. She was still at Justin's house, but it seemed like Justin was gone already. He had probably gone back to being the flamboyant rich businessman that he was. Heather had a lot on her mind, and she simply needed to get the hell out of there. She didn't know what to do about everything, for it meant that she would have to give up one or the other. She wanted to live a normal life and not one that was filled with danger, but she also didn't want to live with a guy who didn't appreciate her for what she was. This was a complete clusterfuck, and Heather didn't know what to make of it.

After she got dressed again, Heather made her way out the door. She felt nervous walking around like this in the broad daylight. Everyone would probably think that she was a cheap prostitute or something, and that was the last thing she wanted to be. She needed to get home fast, but as she walked downstairs she saw Justin waiting for her in the front room.

"Oh good, you're awake. I was hoping that you would

get up soon. I have a meeting in an hour, and I wanted to make sure that I got to see your beautiful face before I left," he said.

Heather smiled weakly but wanted to vomit. This was disgusting, and she needed to get out fast.

"Hey. Listen I'm heading home. I feel gross, and I just need some space. I've had a night," she replied.

"Oh, I know buttercup. I want to see you again soon though. Maybe I can come by your place in a couple days? I would love to take you out on a date too," he said. He looked like an excited puppy dog, and Heather hated that. She felt sick to her stomach, and it wasn't going to be pretty if she told him off right then and there.

"I'll call you to make plans. I'll see you around though," Heather replied. She walked out before Justin could say anything, mentally hoping that her limo driver had stuck around.

Sure enough, he had stuck around like the obedient dog that he was. Heather had a really good driver named Tony, and he was very smart. He also didn't leave unless Heather demanded it, and she knew that he would stay there no matter what. She quickly got in the car and sat there, and Tony looked at her with a wary glance.

"I take it things didn't go so well with you and Justin," he started.

'You're telling me. He's a fucking freak. I don't' want that," she replied.

"I know. Let's go home," he said. Tony knew all about Justin and his fucked up habits. He knew that the guy borderline stalked her all the time, and it was getting pretty old telling him that he couldn't come with her to her hair appointments and other such things. Heather sighed as the driver took her back to her apartment. She got out and looked at him with a smile.

"Thanks for sticking around for me. I don't know what I would do without you," she started.

"I know the feeling. Trust me, he seems like he's a monster. I'm just glad you're safe and you were able to make it out of there," he replied.

Heather nodded and made her way inside. When she got there she flopped down on the couch and started to cry, tears of sadness coursing down her face. She didn't want to be with Justin at all, she wanted Troy. That was who she craved and who she desired, but apparently asking for that was too much. She started to slam her hand against the couch a few times, her tears turning to sobs.

"Why me...why fucking me!" she screamed. She continued to cry for another hour or so before she started to fall asleep. She had a lot to think about, and it would certainly take a lot of time.

The next few weeks were tumultuous, to say the least. Heather hadn't heard a peep from Troy, and it seemed like Justin was being more annoying than usual. He would call her at least five times a day and would leave at least three voicemails. He sent her countless texts, and at one point he came up to her house and started to drive around. It was getting really annoying, and Tony had to shoo him away a couple times just to allow her to get out of there. It wasn't the life that she wanted to live, but it was one that got forced on her to the point where she was completely and utterly miserable about it.

Heather started to feel even worse as time went on. She felt lonely and sad, and it seemed like there was nothing she could do. She wanted to live a normal life, but she was still overcome by sadness and the feeling of loneliness that seemed to course through her body. There was only one person that she wanted, and that was the man that she had fallen for. That was Troy, and she knew that he was the man for her.

The problem was Troy hadn't called her since that night. It seemed like he didn't want to talk and he was completely uncommunicative despite calls and texts. Justin was being borderline stalkerish, but it seemed like Troy didn't want to even give her the time of day. He would see the messages, but he wouldn't even begin to answer them at all. It was annoying as hell, and Heather wished that things would just go the way she wanted them to.

Heather attempted to live a normal life, but it was all for nothing. She wanted to be like the other people, but it seemed like she wasn't able to. She tried to go to other parties that Justin wasn't at, but she felt so distanced from everyone that she definitely didn't want to be a part of it. It made her sad and upset that she seemed to not be able to fit in anywhere and she couldn't even live the life that she wanted.

Thankfully though, her parents didn't seem to be too mad that she left. She lied and told them that she forgot something at home and that she had run out, which was why she was all wet when she came back. Her parents barely believed that, but they let her off the hook. Still, she did worry about what she should do next. She thought that maybe living in the way that she wanted to was good, but it seemed like it wasn't what she really wanted. Heather was so confused, and she felt like a big ball of confusion and worry as she thought about everything that had happened to her over the past few weeks.

One day, Heather got back from the store with her purchases in hand. She wanted to try them on, but she didn't know where to wear them. They weren't suitable for parties, but they weren't good for everyday wear either. It was different than anything she had ever looked at before. She started to try on a corset top along with a leather miniskirt when she heard the door.

"That's odd. Who the hell is that?" she asked herself aloud. She didn't know who could be at her door at this time of day. Justin was still at work and unless he took the day off she wouldn't have to see him. When she got up to the door she looked through the peephole and immediately jumped back and gasped in surprise.

Right in front of her was Troy, and he looked at the door with a curious look on his face. Heather tried to think of what to do next. She could pretend that she wasn't home, but she didn't think that would fly with him. However, she knew the best thing to do was to face the facts, and after a moment she unlocked the door and opened it up slowly.

Troy was there with flowers in his hand. He had an apologetic look on his face, and it seemed different from the normal looks he donned. Heather immediately felt smitten when she looked at the man, and there was no way she could say no to that face.

"Hey there," she said softly. She flushed a little bit as he gazed over her in a longing manner.

"Hey there. Can we talk? I have to discuss some things with you. It's about me. I wanted to tell you these things sooner but I needed some time to think," he replied.

Heather wanted to more than anything, but she didn't know what to say. She had so much on her mind that she didn't know where to go first. However, before she said anything Troy started.

"You look really sexy. I just have to say that first.

Although I would love to do other things, I think we need to have a talk," he started.

"I think so too," Heather replied. They both walked over to the couch and sat on it. Troy cleared his throat, trying to think of the best way to start all of this. After a moment he finally spoke.

"So, about that night...I'm really sorry for the way I acted. I fucking left you, and that hurts me more than anything. I hate thinking about the fact that I left you high and dry, but I didn't know what to do. You looked scared as hell, and you didn't seem to want to be there for me. That's why I told you to leave because I didn't want to hurt you," he explained.

"That makes sense. I mean you did have a pretty scary situation happen," she replied.

"Scary is one way to put it. I prefer to say really fucked up and I want to find the bastard who did it. However, I think I know who it is. But I don't want to stay out there. I can't stay at the place I'm at right now," he replied.

"What do you mean?" she asked.

"I need a place to lie low. I was going to ask you if it was okay to stay here for a bit. I know I'm probably intruding, but I needed somewhere. I'll explain everything," he stated.

Heather didn't know what to do. She really wanted the answers, but at the same time, she didn't know what else to say. She wanted to make him happy, and she did want to keep him safe, but something seemed wrong with it. She felt like there was something wrong with her doing that.

"What do I get out of it? Will it really be everything?" she asked.

"Yes, it will be. Just trust me," he said.

Heather sighed and nodded.

"Thank you. I appreciate it," he said.

"You're welcome. Now, what the hell is going on? I want answers," she stated.

He took a deep breath, trying to keep his composure. However, after a moment he started to cry, his body breaking down from all of the worries that he had.

"I'm sorry Heather. I didn't mean to drag you into this. It's just that I did something bad back in the day, and I didn't know what to do about it. I murdered the head of a rival motorcycle gang, and since then I've been on the run. I've had to do a lot of bad things just to keep myself safe, but I know that after all of that I'm still on the run," he explained.

"What the hell happened?" Heather asked.

"Well, I was ordered to do it. It was supposed to be someone lower than the head, but I ended up getting the wrong guy, and after that, I just lost it. I wasn't able to really do anything, and the motorcycle gang I was with decided to let me go. I was a monster Heather, and then after that, I had to leave. However, it seemed like one of them followed me and I'm in danger. I don't know what to do, and I'm sorry that I dragged you into this. But you have to believe me. This is the truth. I'm not lying to you. Nor would I ever do that," he said.

Heather looked at him with a look of surprise on her face. She needed more information on this. How did he kill a man? How could anyone do that? Heather was left with more questions than answers, and she wanted to know.

Before she could do anything about it, however, she heard a knock on the door, and it sounded just like the knock Justin used.

CHAPTER 3

"WHO THE FUCK IS THAT?" Troy asked. He looked at her with a scared expression on his face and Heather tried to keep calm. She looked at the door and started to slowly creep over to it. The best thing that she could do was at least look at it. If it was someone bad, she would figure out the solution afterward. Right now though, she needed to find a way out fast.

She peered over to see who it was through the peephole. It wasn't Justin, but it was a man who was a lot bigger than she was. He seemed scary, but Heather was willing to take her chances.

"It's a big guy with black hair that's kind of long. Looks scary," she said.

"Oh, that's Charley. Let him in," Troy said. Heather was kind of surprised that a guy like that had such a soft name, but she wasn't going to ask. She opened up the door and looked at the guy, her mind immediately racing.

"Hello there," she said calmly.

"Hey. I'm Charley, one of Troy's friends. Is he here?" he asked.

"Yeah, he is. Why do you care though?"

"I'm one of the former members of his motorcycle club that he was at. I came in to talk to him. It's extremely important that we talk about this right now," he replied.

Heather looked at the man and saw that he was serious. There was no doubt about that, but Heather didn't know if this was worth the risk. Still, she didn't see anything bad about it just yet, and she needed to get more information on just what had happened with Troy. She let him in and he walked over to Troy, giving him a shy smile.

"What's up Char?" Troy asked. He was very friendly with the man and it seemed like Charley was pretty nice to him as well.

"Hey. So there's a small problem, and I felt like talking to you about it now. It involves us and is something that we need to do. Do we need to talk outside?" he asked.

Troy turned to Heather, who had a determined look on her face. There was no way in hell she was going anywhere at this point. She was here for answers, and damn it she was going to get all the answers that she needed.

"Nope. She's with me. She knows a bit about what's going on," Troy explained.

"Well good. I'd feel bad if we had to kick her out of her own house just to talk. Anyway, it's about a rival gang. The new leader knows that you're here. He just came on by and he has guys all around the place. We could leave now, but I think it's best if we have a diversion first. I was thinking of making one with my boys tomorrow, and while that happened we could get out of here," Charley explained.

Troy thought about it, worry on his face. He didn't know if he could leave Heather like this again, but it was something that was pretty bad for everyone.

"Crap. So do they know about Heather?"

"They sure do. That's the biggest issue. I found out who the new leader is and it's someone that I would never expect," Charley replied.

'Who is it?" Troy said. Immediately he thought about it though, and the fear was present on his face.

Charley wanted to tell him, but it looked like he already knew. Heather had a confused look on her face, but Charley just smiled at her.

"Think about it for a bit and you'll know who it is. It's someone important to you," he replied.

Heather didn't know what the hell that meant, and she wished that she could have an explanation for what was going on with everyone. Still, though, it seemed like it was something bad and after a moment or so Troy responded.

"What do you think we should do? He knows about her, and I'm sure that he would be fine with marching right in here as well," Troy stated.

"I know. That's why I'm thinking about the diversion. I would say stay in here and close everything up. I'll make sure that nobody tries to get inside tonight. The rest of the gang members know about this, and they're on your side, Troy. You just have to stay alive for long enough to be there to see them again. That's all that I need you to do," Charley replied.

"Okay," Troy said.

"And you should probably tell Heather about this. Does she know about your past?"

"Kind of. We'll talk after you head out. I think I need to do this in private. Thank you though," Troy said.

"My pleasure. I know exactly how those things are. If something is up let me know and I'll be right on over. You have my number right?"

"Sure do," Troy replied.

"Good. I'll check in on you later. Call me if you need me," Charley said. He walked out before anything else was said. There was nothing but stunned silence between Heather and Troy for a little bit while they tried to think about what the hell had just happened. They definitely didn't know what to think at this point, and it was certainly something that they didn't expect either one of them would be able to face. After a little bit Troy finally responded, trying to break the silence that was between both of them.

"So...what do you think?" he asked.

Heather tried to mull it over but didn't know what the hell to do. She wanted to be with him, but at the same time she was afraid of the consequences. Yet even so, she knew there was no way out of this.

"So he knows who I am right?"

"Yeah. I'm sorry I dragged you into this Heather. I just wanted you. I didn't realize that this was all going to happen," he replied.

Heather felt bad when she heard that. She really wanted to be with him as well, and it hurt her a lot to try and think about the fact that she might not be able to because of this crap. She wanted him, and even though it did worry her, she wanted to at least try.

"What would it take for me to stay with you?" she asked.

"I would say come with me. That's the least that you can do," he replied.

"Then count me in. I want to be with you, and I'm willing to do anything to stay," she replied. Heather knew this was going to be stupid, and it might be the dumbest thing she'd ever done, but she was done with her life. She needed a change and she thought that the best way to have that was to try and be with him.

"Are you sure? It's going to be hard, and we might be on the run for a long time," he admonished.

"I know what I want Troy. I know that deep down you need me. And I need you. You're the only person who's made me feel happy in the last ten years. I've had a lot of shit happen in my life. I was forced to live a life that I never wanted to live, and I was forced into some bullshit-arranged marriage that other people knew was wrong but didn't stand up and say anything about. I was miserable Troy, but you pulled me out of it. You saved me, and I want to be with you to help you as well. I want to save you too, for I know that I can do at least that and maybe something more," she replied. It was true, and when she thought about it, they did need each other. It was what they deserved, and she was going to fulfill the wishes they both had whether it was safe to do so or not. Caution didn't mean jack shit to her at this point, what she needed was him.

"Are you sure that you want to do this? It'll be hard to say the least," he said.

"I know what I want Troy. And I want you," she said simply.

Troy smiled, and before she could say anything else he pressed his lips to hers, kissing them passionately. Immediately Heather responded, her body going crazy with passion and desire. She wanted him more than anything, and as they kissed she knew that it was only going to get better from here.

After a minute or so they pulled away from each other and Troy looked at her with a smile on his face. He started to stroke her cheek, and immediately she flushed crimson.

"You're beautiful you know that?" he said.

"You are too," she replied.

He smiled and pulled away from her, walking around

the apartment. "Pack what you can. Leave whatever is unnecessary at the apartment. However, keep those clothes you have on for later," he cooed.

Heather nodded and packed what she thought she needed. It was almost like she was going on a small vacation, but this one might be for the rest of her life. She didn't care about some of the things in her house. She did grab her phone and laptop in case she needed them, along with some clothes. She noticed that Troy's bike was fixed, and there was a small place to put her luggage. After about an hour, she had everything she needed.

"Do you think we'll ever come back here?" she asked.

"Maybe. After this whole thing blows over we can. Of course, that's up to you. I'll follow you wherever you want," he replied.

Heather nodded, happy that this man gave her so much freedom. She loved it a whole lot, and it was like something, unlike anything she had ever seen before. After a moment, she looked at Troy with a smile on her face, and she pressed her lips to his.

He immediately kissed her back, shocked that a woman like her would ever love him. As he kissed her back, she felt the unbridled passion start to course through her body as she kissed his lips hard. It was nice to feel all of this, and when she opened her mouth slightly she felt his tongue start to snake in there, mingling with hers a little bit. She moaned at the feeling of his mouth against hers, and when his tongue started to do a bit more exploration it made her go crazy. She felt the lust that seemed to course through her body start to get even more prominent, and after a moment she pulled his head down by his hair so that his lips crushed hers and the space between them started to grow less and less. She wanted him, and he wanted her equally as much.

They started to battle with their tongues, each of the muscles moving against one another. Heather moaned, her body going crazy with passion at the way he kissed her. She loved how they lightly ground against one another, both of them moaning in pleasure at the feeling this caused them. Troy was already getting hard, and his hands started to snake behind her body to her backside, lightly grabbing it.

When he did this Heather howled, her body growing hot with pleasure. She wanted him so badly, and Troy wanted her. He started to push his legs apart and then pulled off the corset top that she had on. With a few simple clasps, it was off, leaving her topless. He started to move his hands up to her breasts, lightly kneading them. Heather moaned, her back arching in pleasure as he did this.

Troy had another idea and after a second he fished something out of his pocket. It was a blindfold, something he had always wanted to try before. Heather looked at him with a curious glance, and after a second he pressed it over her eyes.

"Don't worry, I'm going to make you feel great," he said. He started to lightly bite down on her skin, this time leaving marks on purpose. Heather moaned in pleasure as he continued to do this, tracing his teeth and grazing them down to where her breasts were. The sensation was even stronger than before, and she moaned in pleasure at the feeling that he gave her. It was so erotic and sexy that she didn't know what the fuck to do. She was so turned on that Troy smiled, happy that he was able to make her feel like this.

He started to suck on her breasts a tiny bit, letting the nipples harden as he grazed his tongue over them. Heather moaned, her body going crazy with lust and pleasure as he did that. It was so erotic and kinky that it made her go crazy, and she loved the way it felt. It made her so excited that she thought she was going to cum right then and there. She held off though, his hands started to move underneath her skirt. He pushed two of his fingers into her pussy, causing her to moan in pleasure, along with arching her back. He then started to push them in deeper, and the wetness was prominent. He wanted her, and judging by how turned on she was and her ragged breathing, she wanted him as well.

He started to undo his pants, pulling his cock out of them. He then lowered her onto it, and immediately Heather screamed in pleasure. The sensation immediately hit her hard, and after a moment she settled down, getting used to the feeling of him deep inside of her. He started to push her up and down, and Heather moaned at the feeling. She was already so turned on that she could feel her body going crazy with lust and pleasure as he did this. She loved it, and soon she was going faster and faster.

Neither one of them were able to hold on for a long time. Heather was first, and after a few more thrusts she moaned, her body going crazy as her pussy tightened up around his cock. She moaned, her release coming out of her body. Troy soon came as well, his moans of pleasure sounding like music to their ears. They both came almost at the same time, and after he had finished up he pulled Heather off and took the blindfold off of her.

"How was that?" he asked.

"Amazing," she replied.

He smiled at her and gave her a small wink. "Good. Because I only want to give you the best," he replied.

They soon fell asleep together on the couch and Heather felt happier than she ever had before. She loved him, and she knew that it was only a matter of time before she started to fall even further for him.

She loved this bad boy, and she would do whatever she needed for him.

CHAPTER 4

THE NEXT MORNING, Heather and Troy moved out of the house and got on the road. She grabbed whatever she could, but she didn't know what else to take. She thought the essentials were good, and she assumed that she could use her credit card and other things for a little while until her parents caught on and started to cancel them. Thankfully she could use them for now though, for if she didn't she might be screwed over if she needed anything. She took both warm- and cold-weather clothes so that she didn't have to worry about buying anything else for now. She also took the motorcycle clothing that she had got from the store the other day and put it on, marveling at the way she looked.

She did look very sexy in them, and she loved the way Troy looked at her as she wore them. She thought they might be useful, so she packed them along with the other clothing that she planned to wear for the adventure. She didn't know what in the world she was getting into, but she was willing to at least try it out to see what it was that was going to happen to her. Besides, what did she have to lose at

NIGHTRIDER LUSTFUL CRAVING   27

this point? She'd already disappointed her parents, and she didn't want anything to do with the bullshit arranged marriage that they had planned for her. It wasn't going to happen and she was ready to just let it go and move on. If they needed to wait to move on then so be it, but she was going to continue to live her life and have fun regardless of what they said.

When she got up, she saw that Troy was already at the bottom of the stairs of her complex putting the bags in the storage area. He had his own small bag as well, and Heather was a bit shocked at just how small it was. Apparently, that was all that he needed in order to get to where he needed to be. She didn't care though. As long as she had him, she was going to be fine, and in her mind, that was all that mattered.

After locking up her house and saying goodbye to it for the last time, Heather made her way down the stairs to the motorcycle. When she got there she could see some people around the corner, but they didn't attack. Immediately Heather grew nervous as she looked at them, and after a second she took a breath.

"What's going on?" she asked.

"We're being watched by the rival gang. They're probably going to follow us until we get to where we're going to be. Don't worry, I already told my guys here. They'll make sure we can leave the city safely and without any issues whatsoever," he explained.

Heather grew uneasy as she looked around. Was this the best idea? A part of her wanted to back out, to go back to her pathetically normal life that she knew she could handle. This was all way too much for her, and she didn't see how in the world she could survive and keep herself going with all the crap going on. Plus, she felt completely out of the loop when it came to this rival gang, and that was what worried her the most. Troy immediately knew who it was, but she didn't know what to do and how this could affect her. He was worried about her, which is what made her feel worse.

After she got her stuff into the compartment, Troy motioned to her. He was already sitting on his chopper, and while she got on he started the bike. The roar of the engine caused it to come to life, and Heather felt a bit excited. She had never been on a motorcycle like this before, and it seemed like a whole lot of fun. She couldn't wait for what was to come next, and it seemed completely comfortable in her mind. She liked the idea of being on his back too, and as she held onto him, she sighed when she heard the comfortable sound of the wheels starting to move a tiny bit. It was slow at first, but he was going to go faster shortly.

"Hold on to me. Don't let go," he instructed. Heather nodded and held on for dear life as he started to drive away. She looked back, and soon she could see the complex start to fade off into the distance. She felt sad she was leaving this forever, but she also knew that it was for the best. She had to do this for her own sake, and for the sake of Troy and his safety as well. Plus it was an adventure, and she couldn't wait to try it out.

After they drove for a little bit, she could see a couple of other motorcycles in the distance. Troy looked at them and started to speed up. She held on for dear life, their bodies pressing together as they zoomed down the street and continued to follow them, but after a few more twists and turns they were in the clear. There was no one behind them, and they were safe for now. Troy looked at Heather with a smile on his face.

"Don't worry, we're safe now," he bellowed.

Heather nodded as they got on the highway. She held

on for a bit longer, her body comfortable against his. He drove like a real pro, and it was so nice to just sit there and watch him work his magic. It was almost familiar in a way and it made her feel relieved that there was someone out there who gave a damn about her and made sure that her first bike ride was pleasurable.

They were soon on the highway, and then after a bit, they were gone. They were going down one of the express-ways, leaving the city, and then going on the road. As they continued to move for a little bit, Heather started to relax even more. She continued to watch the road as they drove, but she felt a bit sleepy too. However, she kept herself alert for anything that may come up, and so that she didn't fall off or anything.

They continued to drive for about three hours before they reached Arizona. It was big, and Heather felt excited. She had never traveled alone before. Most of the time her parents had kept her on a tight leash, and she never got to have fun like the other kids. She was stuck going on vaca-tions that her parents wanted to go on, and they only took her to Disney once because she wanted to and had begged them to go. She had some nice grades at the time, and that had definitely been an incentive for them to agree as well. Still, she wished she could have had more fun in the past. Now, however, she finally had the chance to and she was happy to have decided to go with it. It seemed like things were going a whole lot better for her, and she definitely liked that. She definitely wanted to stay with Troy, for it felt like she could finally live the life that she'd wanted to. She wanted to see the world from the time she was a little kid, but due to her parents, that was nearly impossible. However, now that she could, she definitely wanted to milk it for all it was worth and she was going to have a great time doing that.

When they got to a small town, Troy stopped at one of the gas stations there. He got out and fueled up, but after he did that, he pulled off his helmet. It was nice to see his face again, for he was behind a mask the majority of the ride. However, now that it was over she could see his happy face, and that made her happier than she had been before.

"Well, we're here. Welcome to my hometown," he said.

Heather looked around a little bit, trying to see what this place was all about. It was nice, and she marveled at the way that looked. However, she felt a bit nervous about it and after a second, she turned back to him.

"Looks great. So what now?"

"Now I think we should check into a motel around here. I think that's our best bet," he explained.

Heather nodded as Troy got back onto the bike. He put his helmet on and started to drive off again. Within five minutes, they were at the motel, and after Troy went in to get a room, he came out to get her.

"I have a room. Let's bring our stuff," he said.

"Sure," she replied. She grabbed her bag and Troy got his. They walked inside, both of them happy to finally be off the road. When they got to the hotel room Heather looked around. It was nice for the price, and she certainly wasn't going to bitch about it. She would rather be in a place like this than anywhere else right now. They put their bags down and Heather got on the bed. Troy laid right next to her and started to stroke her face.

"I'm so happy to have you. Regardless of what happens, I know that I'll always have you and your beautiful face on my side," he said.

"You sure will," she replied. She flushed as he moved

closer to her, their lips merely centimeters from each other. Thankfully, the curtains were closed, for Heather didn't like the idea of having an audience. He placed a chaste kiss on her lips, but Heather immediately wanted more. She started to kiss him hard, causing him to moan in pleasure as she started to kiss him back with much force. It was fun, and he treasured the feeling of her sensual and sexy lips. It felt like a little piece of heaven to him, and Heather felt like she was on cloud nine and living it up as well. It was better than anything she ever felt before, and as they made out Troy started to get on top of her, hovering over her body.

Heather was clad in a pair of simple jeans and a shirt that she had from a while ago. Troy thought she looked dead sexy, and as they kissed, he started to tear the clothes from her body. He then moved his hands down to the button on her jeans and started to pull those off along with her shoes. She was clad in just her underwear for the moment, and Troy smiled as he looked at her.

"You're so damned beautiful," he said.

"You are too," she replied. He lightly caressed her stomach, moving his hand up to her breasts and letting his hand linger there for a second. He then moved up to her cheek and cupped it, looking directly into her eyes. She was amazed at how beautiful he looked as well, for he was definitely very sexy in her mind. It was better than anything she had ever expected, and she felt so at ease as she looked at him.

Troy started to press his lips down her body, leaving a trail of kisses and causing Heather to moan softly at the sheer touch of his lips. It was so sensual, and it definitely didn't feel like anything she had ever felt before. However, when he got to her breasts he moved his hands down to unclasp her bra, pulling it off and causing Heather to moan in pleasure. He then moved his lips over one of her nipples, lightly sucking on it and moving his other hand to play with her other lonely nipple. The two buds were soon very hard, and Heather felt complete and utter pleasure as he touched her. She was already moaning like crazy, and Troy loved to hear it. Her moans were beautiful, just like every other part of her that he loved.

He then moved away and started to pull down her panties, revealing her naked pussy. He would love to fuck that beautiful mound, but this time he wanted to try something else.

"Flip over," he instructed.

Heather didn't know what he was getting at but did so, flipping her body so that her stomach was on the bed and her butt was in the air. Troy started to lightly press his fingers into her entrance behind her pussy, causing a moan to escape her. She had never been touched there by a guy before, and it was definitely very sexy and something that she loved. He then started to push his fingers in slowly, moving them around and making her moan as she felt her back hole expand.

After a moment, he pushed another finger in the hole and then started to scissor them, causing a moan to escape her as he did this. It felt so damned good, and he loved the way she reacted as he did this. He started to move slightly faster in and out of her, causing her to gasp in pleasure. After a moment, he pulled them out and then started to undo his pants.

He pulled off his shirt, revealing his naked chest. He started to slowly pull his pants and boxers down, revealing his thick member that was already hard and ready for her. He grabbed something out of his jacket, which was a small bottle of lube. He coated his cock with it before he pushed himself slowly into her, causing a small gasp of pain as he did this.

Heather had never felt anything like it before. She loved it but at the same time, it did feel a bit awkward, to say the least. She didn't really like the pain, but she was willing to get used to it. Troy pushed himself fully into her and then started to lightly move himself in and out, going slowly, causing small gasps of pleasure to escape her mouth. He then started to move faster and faster, Heather's hole throbbing and her moans growing even louder. She had never been penetrated here, and it was incredible. She like it a lot, and Troy could tell that she definitely liked what he was doing too. She knew that it was only a matter of time before she exploded in ecstasy.

After a few more thrusts, Troy couldn't take it anymore. He was so close, and while he pushed himself into her he started to finger her pussy, causing Heather to moan even louder than she had before. After one last thrust, he gasped, his seed spilling deep into her wet pussy. Heather moaned as she felt her own insides tighten up against his hand, moaning in pleasure once more before she came as well. It was so nice, and she felt even better than she had before.

After he finished up, he pulled out of her, smiling warmly. "Damn that was good," he said.

"Sure was. Thanks, Troy," she replied. She was afraid to say those three words, for it meant that she was finally going to admit something that she wasn't too sure of yet. She wanted to, but at the same time, she didn't know what the implications of saying it to this man were.

"No problem. You're amazing Heather. I am very happy to have you in my life."

Heather smiled and cuddled up to him, thinking about her life. She felt happier than she had for a long while, and her heart was much happier as well. She felt safe around him, and she knew that she wasn't going to leave him no matter what happened to her. She was his, and she was going to stay with him, no matter what obstacles they were faced with.

CHAPTER 5

LATER THAT DAY, Heather and Troy got up from the bed and decided to head over to the base. It was close, but Heather could tell that something was up when they got there. It didn't look too bad, and it seemed like a regular storage warehouse. However, when they got there a man came by and flashed a pistol at him for a second. Troy flashed something from his pocket and the man backed down.

"Shit. Sorry, Troy. How are you?" the man asked. He was very friendly now, and Heather felt a bit awkward when he said those things. Just a minute ago, the man was pushing a pistol into their faces, and now he acted as if they were old chums or something.

"Good Benny. I came to check in with Henry about the whole war going on," he explained.

"Ahh. I thought you were coming for something like that. We were waiting for you. Follow me," he replied.

Troy nodded and started to walk with the man. Heather followed behind, looking around the place. It seemed like your average hideout, but behind every single crate was a man with a gun. She didn't want to feel afraid, but at the same time, she didn't know what to feel exactly. They walked into an office where a man sat. He had a very boyish face and light brown hair. He seemed so young, but when he talked, he had a very old voice that sounded like he was in his thirties.

"Hey there, Troy," he said.

"Hey, Henry. I heard about the issues you've been having. Care to explain?" he asked.

"Sure thing man. Have a seat. And I guess your lady can listen in as well," he said in a reluctant manner.

"Heather can listen in all she wants. She's a part of my life now and she needs to know what's going on," he explained.

"Cool." Heather took a seat nervously next to Troy. He grasped her hand, but that didn't make her feel any better than she had before. She was nervous as shit, and as she looked at the other man he smiled at her.

"No need to get upset, honey. Trust me, I know we look like bad guys but we aren't. We're good men and I think you'll learn very soon what we're all about," he explained.

"She will. Now, what the heck is going on?"

"Well...he's at it again. He's trying to start another goddamn war on our turf. I didn't know how else to reach you, so I had to send Charley over to let you know what the fuck is going on," Henry explained.

"Shit. Really? What's going to happen?"

"I dunno, Troy. But we need your help. You helped us with the war last time, and you're very strong. You need to help us win this; he's looking at your girl too. He knows all about you, and I'm sure that you know this already. I'm just trying to keep you both safe," he explained.

"Thanks, Henry. When does he plan to strike?"

"Probably later today. They were tailing you the entire time, and they're looking for you right now. You have to be very careful Troy, and I think it might be best if we confront him right now on this, just to keep everyone happy," he replied.

Troy looked at Heather, who was worried as hell. He watched her with a serious gaze, and she knew immediately what he was going to say.

"Heather I have to do this. I want to save you babe, and I know that you're definitely strong enough to get through this with me. I love you so much, more than you fucking know. I'm going to do this babe, and I need you to stay with me and watch over my back," he replied.

Heather nodded blankly and Troy managed to give her a small smile. He gave her a kiss and she immediately responded, both of them locked in a passionate embrace for a long moment. After a bit, Henry cleared his throat and the two of them pulled away, looking at the man sheepishly.

"Sorry about that," he said.

"It's cool. I'm used to it, shockingly. Anyway, we could use your help right now. I would appreciate it if we got started with this right away," he replied.

Troy nodded and walked out, leaving Heather all alone. She was scared for him, but a part of her knew that she could trust him no matter what. He loved her, and she knew that the power of love could trump anything.

CHAPTER 6

HEATHER WAITED, and after a minute or so Henry came back. He looked at her with his boyish smile, and in some weird way, she felt like she could totally trust him regardless of what happened.

"Don't worry about them Heather, they'll come out of it alive. I'm sure that Troy will beat that bastard. Besides, he's done it once, and he can certainly do it again," he said.

"What do you mean?"

"Well a while back, Troy had a very bad vendetta against him so he went after the guy. However, instead of getting the guy that he wanted, he attacked the leader instead. Did he tell you why he left us in the first place?"

Heather shook her head. "Not entirely. It seemed a bit weird though."

"It was. Well, he caused some serious shit with these guys and that caused the other guy to blow up and say that he would kill him if he got a chance. Troy didn't want to take the risk, so he left town. However, what he didn't know was that this guy had a strong idea of where he was going, so he went back to his parent's house. When he got there, he saw you and now he knows a whole lot about you. And when he heard you were seeing Troy he immediately knew where he was. He used you to get to him, and that's why Troy hates this guy so much," the man explained.

"Shit that's crazy," Heather said. She fiddled with the chair seat, looking around.

"Well, I can show you what's going on outside if you'd like. There is a lot of shit going down though. I know they're attacking our base right now, and I think Troy is getting ready to take that guy out," Henry said.

"Let's go see," she said. She didn't care about the bloodshed at all, as long as Troy was safe. They went outside, and she looked around the place. It was crazy, and Heather almost felt sick to her stomach at what she saw.

This wasn't some ordinary little playground war where people used their fists. No, this was a turf war with guns and other such things. She could see a couple of bombs going off too, and she could hear the agonized screams from both sides. She looked to see if Troy was out there, but he wasn't just yet.

"Where's Troy?" she asked.

"He's not coming out yet until he sees the boss here. That's who he wants. He doesn't give two shits about the small fry. He wants the leader and wants to get his revenge on him," he explained.

Heather really wanted to know who the leader was. It was something that ate at her and made her wonder. She felt super nervous about what was about to happen, and she was still in suspense. She needed to know, and after a little bit, she finally got her answer.

She saw Troy start to leave, and she could see that he was suited up. He looked so different. He wasn't the quiet and mysterious man that she knew and loved. This man was a leader and he was bent on making sure that people knew that. When he got up to where the edge of his turf was, he stood there. There was another man who came by, and when he reached Troy, he said something. Heather couldn't make out what it was, but when he uttered it, everyone stopped dead in their tracks. He looked over at Troy and Heather gasped at whom it was.

Right in front of Troy was Justin, and he had a gun in his hands, glaring at Troy with a malicious look on his face.

CHAPTER 7

HEATHER WANTED to try to stop them but as she did, Henry held her back.

"Stop. This is their fight," he explained.

However, the sound caused Justin to look up, and when he saw her he immediately grinned.

"I didn't know your little girlfriend and my fiancé was going to be here," he said angrily.

"Shut up Justin. She's not yours," Troy replied.

"Oh, bullshit. She was mine way before you came around. She loves me, and she wants to marry me. Of course, that's what her parents think, and they have the final say in who she marries. She would never be allowed to marry a man like you. You're too rough, and they wouldn't like an uncouth man to take care of their lovely daughter," he said.

"Shut up Justin. Like you're any better," he said.

"Actually I am. I'm a good man and I can take care of her. And if she says no I'll kill her on the spot right now," he replied. He aimed the gun straight at Heather's face, and she tried to hide but wasn't able to. One wrong move and she was history.

"Don't mess with her, Justin. You're my enemy, not hers," he said.

"True. I can get her once we're done here. Not that you're going to live or anything of course," he replied. He started to lunge at Troy and Troy dodged the move, landing an elbow right in the man's gut. Justin tried to sweep his leg, and after two unsuccessful attempts, he was able to do it. Troy fell to the ground and Justin came over, the gun pressed right against his neck.

"Do you really think you can leave this? You're nothing but a pathetic little man who can't get what he wants. I can have whatever I desire, including the woman who loves you. You're a failure Troy, and you're pathetic, to say the least," he stated.

Heather wanted to scream out to Troy, but Henry held her arm to silence her. She was so angry, and just looking at him made her rage.

"Fuck, what do I do?" she said.

"Just watch, Heather. He'll get out of this," he said.

"But how? And how in the world did Justin become a gang leader? Why the hell would he do that?" she asked in a very forthright manner. It seemed so weird that he would waste his time with something like that. Then again, it was Justin and he was a weird fucker, to say the least.

"I don't know. But don't worry about them. He was a gang member who came into money when he found out about his real parents. He was an orphan for the longest time, and then when he found them they gave him a ton of money. That's how he came to be the rich bastard he is today. He probably then heard about your family and wanted to marry you so that he could become even richer than before," he replied.

"This man is a fucking monster," she said.

"I know. But don't worry about that. Worry about what's happening down there," he said. Heather watched as Troy moved away, getting up and hitting Justin in the stomach once again. They each took hits, both of them falling to the ground and getting into bad positions, but it seemed like they were able to get out of them easily. However, after one wrong move Justin fell to the ground, and before he could get back up Troy grabbed the gun and shot him point-blank in the face.

It was an immediate kill, and Heather's eyes widened as she saw what happened. She had never seen a guy kill someone in real life, and it seemed a whole hell of a lot scarier in real life than it did in any video game. This wasn't some sort of fake reality show, this was the truth and Justin was gone.

Troy moved away, breathing heavily from his place on the ground. He turned to Heather with a small smile on his face. She immediately ran over to him, embracing him hard.

"You're safe," she said. She was so happy that he was alive. Even though she did have a past with Justin, she didn't like the way he treated her and everyone else. He had got what he deserved, and if he had to go six feet under then so be it.

"Holy shit, you are too," he replied. It seemed almost surreal for him to say that. He thought for sure that he was a goner. However, he had her and she had him, and after a bit, they pulled away. They had defeated Justin, and it was a victory that both of them could be happy over.

Troy looked a bit bloodied, and looked as though he needed a little bit of medical attention on his face. Heather grabbed him and carried him inside. There was a member there who was a trained doctor and after a bit, he had Troy all cleaned up and happy. Troy was thankful that he was alive, and Heather was so happy too. They had won the war, and now that Justin was gone, they didn't have to worry about anything.

Heather thought about what this could mean for her. She could finally go back to her old life without any issues. Of course, there might be some issues with the fact that Justin was dead now, but she could work to resolve them. She could also live with Troy without any issues, and that was something that made her a whole lot happier than she had ever been before. Things were finally going her way, and she could be happy as a clam now that she had him and she was able to successfully live the life that she wanted without any issues at all.

After they got Troy patched up he looked at Heather with a small smile on his face. He extended his hand and looked at her with his beautiful dark eyes.

"Come with me. I want to ask you something privately," he said. Heather nodded and walked with him to where he was going. She didn't know what to expect, but when she got to the balcony where she and Henry had watched the whole battle unfold, he looked at her with a smile on his face.

Instead of saying anything, he got down on one knee and looked at her with a grin on his face. He pulled some-thing out of his pocket and when Heather saw it, she gasped. It was a ring, and it shone in the moonlight. It was very pretty, and it was definitely something that she had never expected to ever get from him.

"Heather. I love you. I feel bad that I haven't said that as much as I've wanted to. However, I'm ready to confront it and say it now. Will you marry me?" he asked.

Heather was in shock. She didn't know what to say. She knew what the answer was. And it was definitely something that she wanted to say. She wanted to be his, and that was something that she craved more than anything right now.

"I feel honored Troy. I will marry you. And I love you too," she said.

Troy smiled and pulled her close to him, kissing her senseless. She immediately responded, her body and mind happy with the way things were going. She had never felt this good before, and the fact that a man cared about her like this was something to really marvel at. She loved it, and she knew that this was the start of something new.

After they broke away, Troy placed the ring on her finger, smiling at her with a cheeky grin.

"There you are, babe. Now let's go plan our wedding shall we?"

CHAPTER 8

HEATHER KNEW WHAT SHE WANTED. She wanted a very private marriage with nobody to bother her. She didn't even want her parents to attend, and the only people that would be there were the members of the motorcycle gang. It worked out for them, for they were happy that Troy found love as well. It seemed that he had had some issues with women in the past. However, now that it was resolved, Heather felt happier than she had ever felt before, and she was definitely going to love this more than anything she had ever experienced. She was so happy, and it seemed that Troy was happy for her as well.

They had a little makeshift altar, where one of the members did the wedding. He used to be a priest until he got into some trouble, and now he was a member of the gang. He was a very cool guy, and after a few hours, Heather appeared for her wedding in a white dress that she had packed. It was small, but it did the trick. Troy was in nothing but a small pair of leather pants and a leather vest. It wasn't a traditional wedding, that's for sure.

When they got there, they both walked up, and the man

looked at them with a smile on his face. He had never seen anything like this before. Even though it did seem a bit odd, he knew that love is love and if they were happy and wanted to be with each other he wasn't going to stop them.

Heather looked at Troy, who seemed happy. He already had the wedding rings planned, so she hadn't really worn her engagement ring for very long. She hadn't even told her parents about this, and she definitely didn't know how to approach this subject with them. She wanted to be with Troy, and nothing was going to stop her now. If they got mad and got rid of her, then so be it. She knew that they didn't really love her the way that she had thought they did, so it wouldn't be any love lost.

When she got up there, Troy looked at her and gave her a warm smile. It was so nice to see, like a refreshing breeze on a hot day. He seemed to be happier than anything she had ever seen before, and he had a giant grin that she had never seen on his face ever. This was better than sex in his mind, for he could finally have the woman that he'd wanted for the longest time.

The man looked at them with a smile before starting to lead them through their vows. "Alright. We are gathered here tonight to wed these two in holy matrimony. If there is anyone who is against this, please speak now or forever hold your peace," he said. None of the members spoke, so he took that as a no when it came to the answer to his statement.

"Good. Now I want you to put the ring on her finger Troy," the man said. Troy did so, his mind racing and his face looking a little nervous as he put the ring on her dainty finger.

"Good. Now you do the same Heather," he instructed. Heather did as well, smiling warmly at the man that she could finally call her husband. It was definitely something that she had never thought would happen in her life. Plus she was going to be happy in her marriage, another big thing that she had thought she could never have.

"Alright. Now you two may kiss, and I properly pronounce you husband and wife," he said. Troy pulled her in and gave her a big and sloppy kiss, and all of the guys started to cheer happily. It was nice to have so much support, and Heather felt happier than she had ever felt before. This was almost like a high, and she knew that she wasn't going to come down. She was so happy, and the wedding was short and sweet.

After they broke away, they looked at all of their friends and proceeded out. They didn't even think of reception or anything, for there was only one thing on their mind. They wanted to express their love to each other right then and there, and although they wished they could celebrate it with each other, they had other plans in mind. They wanted to consummate their marriage right away, regardless of what everyone else wanted them to do.

The bike was waiting for them, and Troy and Heather took it immediately to the hotel. One of them suggested they could drive when Troy told them about the engagement and marriage, but Troy blatantly refused that. He wanted to take her home on his bike, and Heather was completely okay with that. It seemed romantic in a way, and she felt like a princess when he did these things for her. She had never felt so damned happy in her life.

The drive was very fast, and they were soon back at the motel. Troy quickly got the door open, and when he did, Heather came in. He pushed her down on the bed, kissing her senseless. Heather immediately responded, kissing him hard as well. It was so nice, and she felt super happy that this was the man she could call her husband.

Heather had always thought she was going to hate her husband. With the track record of relationships she had had in the past, including the arranged marriage between her and Justin, she thought that she could never be happy in a relationship. She felt like it was some sort of far-off desire, something that she could never have due to the circumstances that she had been given. However, Troy seemed to prove all of that wrong in the best way possible. He showed her that marriage and relationships could be fun, and not just something that she had to do because she was forced to by Mommy and Daddy. This was a dream come true, and Troy was happy at the way she responded to him as well. She was happy, and he could feel the passion start to get even bigger and more pronounced. Nothing could stop them now, for they were in love and they would be able to achieve all of the goals that they had set for themselves, and they could certainly have the ability to be happy with each other in the best ways possible.

Troy felt so happy that as he kissed her he wasn't able to hold back. They were locking lips constantly, and while they did that, they hugged each other hard, both of them bent on not letting the other go. They weren't ever going to get rid of each other, and they knew that they would never get tired of either of their bodies ever. Troy loved how beautiful she was, and Heather loved how sexy and seductive he was. He was the tall, dark, and handsome man that she wanted, and she felt like she was completely satisfied just by kissing this man.

As they kissed each other hard, Heather felt her pussy grow wet. She only had on a skin-colored thong, and even that was starting to get soaked by her own personal pleasure and desires. Troy knew what to do next, and after that, he pulled away and smiled at her with a warm grin.

"Looks like someone needs a bit of a release," he said.

"I would love it," she replied.

"Well let me strip you first, and then we can have some real fun," he said in a devilishly sexy way. He was so hot, and just looking at him made her go completely and utterly mad. He started to pull off her dress, sliding it down her shoulders and off her small body, revealing her naked breasts. Troy lightly touched and licked both of them, causing the moans that he loved so much to escape her mouth. She was so horny that she had trouble trying to control herself at that moment, and it was only a matter of time before her desire for release got even bigger. She wanted him so badly, and Troy knew this. He was ready to give her what she wanted, and he definitely wanted to make her happy as well.

He started to move his hands to her thong, lightly touching and grazing his hand in a languid manner over the area. Heather moaned, her body arching in pleasure as he lightly grazed over the sensitive area. It felt so good, and as he did this, he could see the pleasure present in her eyes. It was so erotic that he loved the way she looked, and after a little bit, he knew exactly what he wanted. He started to lightly tug on the thong, pulling it down to reveal her naked pussy. He then pushed his face close to it, smelling her tantalizing body.

"You smell amazing. I bet you taste as good as you smell," he said in a very sexy manner. Heather nodded as he started to extend his tongue and lightly touch the tip of her clitoris.

Heather hadn't ever felt this good before, and as he touched her there she felt like she was about to go crazy. It felt so damned good, and as he did it, he watched as she gasped and lightly gripped the sheets. He continued to do it, loving the way that she looked when he started to play with her. It was so erotic and sexy that he didn't know what to do with himself. He wanted to continue eating her out, but his cock was growing bigger just from touching her and hearing her moans. He decided to delve in a bit deeper, touching her pussy a bit more and causing her to go even crazier than he had ever seen her go. He started to lightly play with her pussy while he licked her fervently, and after a few more minutes of doing that, he knew that Heather couldn't take it anymore. It was so sexy and erotic to watch her, but he knew that all good things must come to an end. He needed to be inside of her, and that's exactly what he was about to do.

After he finished, he pulled away and then started to pull down his leather pants. His cock was already feeling uncomfortable as he pulled it out, but then when it sprang free he gasped in pleasure. It was nice to feel, and after a second he positioned himself inside of her, pushing himself in and out rough and hard.

He started at a slow pace, but then after a bit, he started to move faster and faster. Heather moaned, her body going crazy with lust as he did this. Troy started to move faster and faster, loving the way her tight pussy seemed to take all of him in and make him feel amazing. He then started to angle his body in a different manner, hitting her directly in her sweet spot. The minute he hit that he knew it was all over for her, and he could feel her pussy walls tighten up against his cock.

After a few more thrusts Heather gasped, her body tightening up and then releasing her essence. It felt amazing, and after she did that Troy groaned, his cock releasing its seed into her body. It was the best sex they had ever had, and Heather was so happy with how nice it felt.

After he finished up, he pulled out of her and looked at her with a cheeky grin. She smiled back at him with an equally cheesy smile.

"I love you Heather. And I'm happy to have you as my wife," he said.

"I'm happy to have you too, Troy," she replied. They started to fall asleep on the bed and Heather knew this was what she wanted. She was finally free, and that was something better than anything she had ever felt before.

ABOUT THE AUTHOR

Candra Aubrey is an emerging erotica author of many erotica kinks and sub-genres. Be sure to check out other books and leave a review if this story got you hot!

Visit my blog at Candra Aubrey's Blog

Join my newsletter for the exclusive Candra Aubrey's Newsletter

Sign up for Free Stories from Xplicit Press Authors

Xplicit Press Author Updates

Like Xplicit Press on Facebook

Follow Xplicit Press on Twitter

Readers: I want to expand a few of the stories to see where the characters can be explored further. If there are any of the stories that you would like to read more about again, I'd love to hear from you!

Keep In Touch
Candra Aubrey
info@candraaubrey.com